D1030402

Behavior MATTERS

MONKEY NEEDS TO LISTEN

WRITTEN BY SUE GRAVES

ILLUSTRATED BY TREVOR DUNTON

WINDMILL BOOKS

Published in 2017 by **Windmill Books**, an Imprint of Rosen Publishing
29 East 21st Street, New York, NY 10010

Series Editor: Jackie Hamley
Series Designer: Cathryn Gilbert

Cataloging-in-Publication Data

Names: Graves, Sue. | Dunton, Trevor, illustrator.

Title: Monkey needs to listen / by Sue Graves; illustrated by Trevor Dunton.

Description: New York : Windmill Books, 2016. | Series: Behavior matters | Includes index, table of contents, and glossary.

Identifiers: ISBN 9781499480900 (pbk.) | ISBN 9781499480832 (library bound) | ISBN 9781499480702 (6 pack)

Subjects: LCSH: Listening--Juvenile literature. | Behavior--Juvenile literature.

Classification: LCC PZ7.G7754 Mo 2016 | DDC [F]-dc23

Manufactured in the United States of America

CPSIA Compliance Information: Batch #BS16PK: For Further Information contact Rosen Publishing, New York, New York at 1-800-237-9932

CONTENTS

Mr. Croc was very busy. He was in the shed at Jungle School. He was trying to think of some good ideas for the After School Club. Mr. Croc was in charge of the After School Club.

He liked to think of **interesting** and **exciting** things for everyone to do. He found some old wheels and some wood. The wheels and the wood gave him a **good idea**. He went to tell everyone about it.

Mr. Croc told everyone to sit still and to listen. Everyone sat still and listened carefully. But **Monkey did not sit still** and he **did not listen**. Mr. Croc told everyone his good idea.

He told them they were going to work in **teams**. He said each team was going to build a go-kart out of the wood and the wheels. He said that when the go-karts were finished, they would race them around the swamp.

Then Mr. Croc asked who would like to **drive** the go-karts. Everyone wanted to drive them. Everyone put up their hands. Mr. Croc had a good idea. He put everyone's names in a hat.

First he pulled out Elephant's name. Elephant was very **excited**. Then he pulled out Monkey's name. He told Monkey that he was going to drive a go-kart, too. Monkey was very excited.

Mr. Croc said that everyone needed to listen to the instructions. He said it was important to listen carefully. He said everyone had to work as a **team**. They had to work together to build the go-karts. He said they had to check they were **safe** to race, too. Everyone listened carefully. But Monkey **did not listen** at all.

Then Mr. Croc gave everyone special jobs to do. Lion had to **build** the go-kart. Hippo had to **put on** the wheels. Little Lion had to **fix** the steering wheel.

Monkey had to **check** the wheels and the steering wheel. Mr. Croc said it was important to check them carefully to make sure the go-kart was safe to race. But Monkey **did not listen**.

Soon the go-kart was ready. Hippo had to **remind** Monkey to check the wheels. But Monkey **did not listen**.

Little Lion had to **remind** Monkey to check the steering wheel. But Monkey **did not listen**.

Soon it was the day of the race. Everyone was excited. Monkey and Elephant lined up at the start. Mr. Croc said they needed to listen to the instructions. He told them **not** to go **too fast** around the corner of the swamp. But Monkey **did not listen**. He sped off in his go-kart.

Monkey went **too fast** around the corner of the swamp. The wheels began to **wobble** ... and the steering wheel began to **shake!**

Suddenly the steering wheel broke off. The go-kart began to **skid**. Then it shot up into the air. It spun around and around and then ... it shot into the swamp with a loud **PLOP!**

Everyone ran to help Monkey. They pulled him out of the swamp. He was very wet and smelly. Then they pulled out the go-kart. It was bent and twisted. Mr. Croc was **upset**. "**Monkey needs to listen!**" everyone said.

Monkey was sorry that he **had not listened**. He was sorry that he had **not checked** the wheels and the steering wheel. He was sorry that he had gone **too fast**. Worst of all, he was **sorry** that he had crashed and **spoiled** the race for everyone.

Then Elephant had a **good idea**. He asked Mr. Croc if everyone could help fix Monkey's go-kart. He asked if they could race the go-karts again when it was fixed. Mr. Croc said it was a very good idea.

Everyone helped to fix Monkey's go-kart. Everyone worked together as a **team**. This time Monkey **listened carefully**.

Hippo did not have to remind him to check the wheels. He was **pleased**. Little Lion did not have to remind Monkey to check the steering wheel. He was **pleased**.

Soon it was time to race the go-karts. Everyone was excited. Monkey and Elephant lined up at the start. Mr. Croc told everyone to **listen** to the instructions. He told them not to drive too fast around the corner of the swamp. This time Monkey listened.

25

Monkey raced hard. But this time he did not go too fast around the corner of the swamp. This time the wheels **did not wobble** and the steering wheel **did not shake**. Best of all the go-kart **did not skid**.

Monkey and Elephant raced over the finish line together. Everyone clapped and cheered!

Note About Sharing This Book

The ***Behavior Matters*** series has been developed to provide a starting point for further discussion on children's behavior both in relation to themselves and others. The series is set in the jungle with animal characters reflecting typical behavior traits often seen in young children.

Monkey Needs to Listen

This story looks at the importance of listening to instructions and the problems that can arise when someone doesn't listen – from spoiling others' fun and ruining their efforts, to potentially putting themselves and others at risk.

How to use the book

The book is designed for adults to share with either an individual child, or a group of children, and as a starting point for discussion.

The book also provides visual support and repeated words and phrases to build reading confidence.

Before reading the story

Choose a time to read when you and the children are relaxed and have time to share the story.

Spend time looking at the illustrations and talk about what the book might be about before reading it together.

Encourage children to employ a phonics first approach to tackling new words by sounding the words out.

After reading, talk about the book with the children:

- What was the story about? Talk about the consequences of Monkey's behavior. Why do the children think it is important to pay attention when instructions are being given?

- Have the children ever failed to listen to instructions from a teacher, a parent or a guardian? What happened? What were the consequences? Encourage the children to speak about their own experiences.

- Extend this by asking the children if they have experienced problems resulting from someone else not listening or following instructions? How did they feel towards the person who did not listen? What happened?

- Discuss ways of helping the children to concentrate and to listen carefully while instructions are being given. Examples might be to sit still and to hold your hands together so that you don't fidget, to focus on the instructor, and so on.

- Encourage listening to instructions by playing a simple game with the children such as "Simon Says." Remind the children of the rules of the game and point out that they must do exactly what Simon says unless the instruction is not prefixed with the words "Simon says…!"

Glossary

excited having very strong feelings about something

good idea a good plan or action

instructions plans to complete something

listen to pay attention when people are talking

sit still to stay in one place

sorry to regret or be sad about something you did

team people working together to reach a goal

For More Information

Burton, Linda. *Pay Attention, Emily Brown!* Bethesda, MD: Woodbine House, 2011.

Cook, Julia. *The Worst Day of My Life Ever!* Boys Town, NE: Boys Town Press, 2011.

Lester, Helen. *Listen, Buddy*. New York: Houghton Mifflin Harcourt, 2013.

INDEX